Rocket
and the
Perfect Pumpkin

Copyright © 2020 by Tad Hills
Text by Elle Stephens
Art by Grace Mills

All rights reserved. Published in the United States by Schwartz & Wade Books, an imprint of Random House Children's Books, a division of Penguin Random House LLC, New York.

Schwartz & Wade Books and the colophon are trademarks of Penguin Random House LLC.

Visit us on the Web! rhcbooks.com

Educators and librarians, for a variety of teaching tools, visit us at RHTeachersLibrarians.com

Library of Congress Cataloging-in-Publication Data is available upon request.
ISBN 978-0-593-17788-4 (hardback) | ISBN 978-0-593-17786-0 (hardcover library binding) | ISBN 978-0-593-17787-7 (ebook) | ISBN 978-0-593-17785-3 (paperback)

The text of this book is set in 28-point Century.
The illustrations are digitally rendered.

MANUFACTURED IN CHINA

1 3 5 7 9 10 8 6 4 2

First Edition

Rocket
and the
Perfect Pumpkin

Pictures based on the art by Tad Hills

schwartz **&** wade books • new york

It is fall!

"Do you want to find
a pumpkin with me,
Rocket?" Bella asks.

"Yes!" Rocket says.
"Today is the perfect day
to find a pumpkin!"

Rocket and Bella
go up the hill
to the pumpkin patch.

The pumpkin patch
is full of pumpkins!

Some are big.

Some are small.

Some have bumps.

Some have spots.

There are so many

shapes and sizes!

Rocket sees a pumpkin
he likes.
It is big, round,
and very orange.

"It is the perfect pumpkin!" says Bella.

The pumpkin is
too heavy to carry!

Rocket and Bella
push and push.

The pumpkin starts
to roll.

They push and push.
The pumpkin rolls faster.

"Oh, no!" says Rocket.

The pumpkin
is getting away.

Rocket and Bella run
down, down, down
the hill.

The pumpkin rolls
down, down, down
the hill.

The pumpkin
bumps into
Mr. Barker's house.

Mr. Barker wakes up.

Mr. Barker is not happy.

Bark! Bark! Bark!

He sniffs the pumpkin.
It is big, round,
and very orange.

Rocket and Bella reach
Mr. Barker's house.
"Sorry!" Bella says.
"Our pumpkin got away."

"That is a perfect pumpkin!"
Mr. Barker says.

"You may have it!"
says Bella.

"Yes, it is for you!"
Rocket agrees.

Mr. Barker loves
his pumpkin.
He is very happy.

"Making friends happy
feels even better
than having a
perfect pumpkin,"
says Rocket.

"Yes," Bella says.
"Making friends happy
feels great indeed."